SUMMER LOVE

Sapphic Mountain, Book Two

Gemma Addison Dove

CONTENTS

ABOUT THE BOOK

Samantha is a reclusive mountain woman, and that's just fine with her. But Samantha's sister, Mallory, drags the stoic mountain woman out of her cabin and forces her to attend Camp Pride's staff party. Samantha's old high school sweetheart has returned to the tiny mountain town to work at the summer camp as an art teacher. Sparks fly between Samantha and Caroline, their old flame quickly rekindling. But Caroline will only be in town for two months, so they agree to have a no strings attached summer fling. No one's ever had problems with that arrangement, right?

Summer Love is a steamy sapphic instalove short romance novella featuring a mountain woman and a cute art teacher finding true love. It is the second book in the *Sapphic Mountain Collection*, and while all of the stories are standalones, it is better to read them in order.

This novella contains mature themes and is intended for mature, adult audiences.

This quick read includes:

- Sapphic/Lesbian romance.

- Low angst instalove short romance.

- Sweet but steamy.

- Reunited high school sweethearts.

- Both characters are in their thirties.

- Mountain Woman + Art Teacher.

- Soft Butch + Femme.

- No strings attached summer fling.

- (or so they think)

- Can be read as a standalone.

A Note from the Author

This is a work of fiction. All characters are over eighteen and are consenting adults. There are no family relations between characters. This is a steamy sapphic romance with mature themes and is intended for readers eighteen or older. No AI was used to assist in writing this story, and no AI was used by the cover designer for this book.

CHAPTER ONE: SAMANTHA

I pulled into the driveway of my mountain home, noting my sister's truck already parked out front. I let out a long sigh. It's not that I don't want to see her, but I just finished a long and boring shift with Mountain Rescue. In this business, a slow day is a good day. It means I didn't have to help a lost family of hikers or do any daring rescues, but it makes for a very long, boring shift. I just want to go home, eat dinner, and be entertained by a movie, or maybe read a book. Alone.

"Mallory? Hello?" I call as I enter the cabin. Cabin might not be the right word for it, since it's our old family home and the size of a large house, but it's built like a rustic log cabin.

"Hey big sis," Mallory says from where she sits at the kitchen island, looking up from her phone. She's wearing her long brown hair in a ponytail, the complete opposite of my short blonde pixie cut. "It's Camp Pride's Pre-Opening Staff Party tonight. I'm here to pick you up so you can make it in time for dinner. If I show up in person, you can't ignore my calls or texts and pretend like you didn't know it was tonight."

I scowl. "I never go to your camp staff parties. I'm not part of your staff."

"Yes, but it's technically a family business, so you're always invited," she insists. "Go wash up and put something nice on. You have twenty minutes."

"I'm not going," I insist.

"What exactly are your plans tonight, Samantha?" Mallory asks. "Eat dinner alone? You need to get out more often."

"I get out and about for work five days a week," I argue. "I'm out and about all over this mountain!"

"You drive around in a truck all by yourself," she counters.

"I'm on patrol," I say. "Soon enough, summer will be in full swing, and this mountainside will be crawling with tourists, and then I'll be talking to people every day."

"It's not the same," Mallory says. "Please. Just come to the party. Nelly and Lora will be there."

She names our younger sister and her new wife, Lora, who also happens to be my best friend. It was a bit of a shock when those two decided to be together, but seeing how well they compliment each other makes me happy for them.

"Mallory…" I say, letting out a long sigh. "I'm fine on my own."

Mallory frowns. "But Nelly and I worry about you. It'd make both of us happy if you just came and spent some time with us."

"Spending time with you and Nelly and your partners is fine," I say. "It's just the rest of the party that's not my thing."

"Just come to this one little camp party, and I promise not to bother you with social events for the entire rest of the summer," Mallory says. She holds out her hand to me, ready to shake.

"Promise?" I ask. "Not a single summer event. Nothing. At all. All Summer."

"I promise," Mallory says. "Deal or no deal?"

If going to this one little dinner party is all it takes to get her off my back for the rest of the summer, then it sounds like a pretty good compromise.

I shake her hand: "Deal."

Twenty minutes later, I've showered and changed. My short hair is still a bit damp, but I roll my window down, letting the wind tousle it and help dry it. I've put my best dark wash jeans on and my favorite blue plaid shirt, which Mallory deemed good enough for a dinner at a campground. I'm following in my truck behind Mallory as we head up the mountain to Camp Pride. Our parents used to run the camp, and after they passed away, it was shut down for a few years. But Mallory and her husband Steve have been running it for the past three years and they seem to get more campers, and subsequently more staff, every single summer. Before the campers arrive, Mallory and Steve always host a welcome party for their staff, as well as a week of in-person training. I went to their dinner party their first year, to help celebrate the re-opening of the camp, but haven't been since. Big parties full of people I don't know are not exactly my idea of a good time. Everything is always a little bit too loud, too busy, too...everything. It gives me a headache.

I pull into the gravel camp parking lot behind Mallory and follow her to the outdoor eating area. There are rows of colorful painted picnic tables and lights strewn from tree to tree.

Mallory's husband Steve and Nelly's wife Lora are currently handling the two barbecues they have set up, along with some teenagers I don't recognize, who are probably new camp counselors. My sister Nelly is arranging desserts on a table next to the barbecue. She's unpacking several boxes of cupcakes. The cupcakes are all topped with sky blue icing and little candy rainbows. Nelly's a baker by trade, so I know the cupcakes are going to be delicious. I walk over, fully intending to swipe one and eat my cake before dinner, just to make sure I don't miss out.

"Samantha!" Nelly says and runs around the table so she can hug me. "You're here!"

"Yeah, I'm here," I say. "Can I have a cupcake?"

"It's dessert," she says. "But of course. Help yourself."

I pick one out and bite into it, savoring the sweet goodness.

"Amazing, as always," I tell my baby sister.

"Thank you," she says, then goes back to unpacking the rest.

I offer to help, seeing as she still has three unpacked boxes.

"Why so many?" I ask.

"This is the camp's biggest year yet," Steve says from the barbecue next to us. "We have *double* the number of campers from last year. We're finally at full capacity. Every cabin and every bed is full. We've also had to hire more staff than usual, making this our biggest pre-opening staff party yet."

"Wonderful," I say. On the one hand, yes, I'm happy for the camp being full and business doing well. On the other hand: I'm here, at this party; the biggest staff party they've ever thrown. I can already feel a headache creeping in. Nelly catches my eye and gives me an apologetic smile and bumps her elbow against mine.

"I'm glad you're here, Sam," she says. "I feel like I never see you anymore."

"You spend a lot of time in town for work and I spend a lot of time on the mountain," I say with a shrug. "But it's nice seeing you, Nelly."

I set down the last cupcake in the display and then look up to survey the crowd of staff that's milling around the picnic tables. And then I see her: the dark red curls, her bright green eyes, and her bare, freckled shoulders being shown off by the pretty blue, sleeveless sundress she's wearing. She catches my eye and smiles broadly, and I feel like the entire party has frozen. It's *her*. It's Caroline, the girl I dated in high school. Well, dated is probably not the right word. The girl I fooled around with in high school is probably a more appropriate statement. The girl who was my first kiss, my first...*everything*. And the only person I've ever been in love with.

Chapter Two: Caroline

Samantha locks eyes with me and looks absolutely shocked to see me. I swallow the nervous lump that has risen in my throat, and I pull my eyes away from the tall, blonde mountain woman. I quickly find Mallory and give her my best glare possible. Judging by Samantha's utterly shocked expression, she had no idea I was going to be here.

Mallory saunters over, grinning. "What?"

"You didn't tell her," I say, grabbing her by the arm and turning my back on Samantha.

"I may have left it out while dragging her here," Mallory says.

"Why didn't you tell her?" I ask.

"Because if she knew her old high school flame was going to be here, she *never* would have come," Mallory says. "I had a hard enough time getting her here as it is. She hates these things."

Samantha *definitely* hates these things: big parties, formal gatherings, *high school prom*. I wanted her to be my date for prom, way back when, and she absolutely refused. Back then, I wasn't sure if it was the actual social gathering, or if she wasn't quite ready to fully come out as a lesbian, or if she just...wasn't that interested in me beyond our physical relationship and didn't want to make it official by being prom dates. But none of that ended up mattering, because she flat out turned me down, I never prodded for answers, and then I got a scholarship to the Rhode Island School of Design for their Illustration program. I haven't been back to my small hometown of Blytheton since.

"If she hates these things, then why did you make her come?" I ask Mallory.

"She's determined to be a reclusive, grumpy mountain woman," Mallory says. "But I know her better than that. She doesn't really want to be alone. She has so much love to give. She raised me and Nelly after our parents died, and she pretty much gave up on her own hopes and dreams, sacrificing everything for us. But now we're all grown up and Nelly and I are both happily married. So, now it's Sam's turn to fall in love."

I feel my cheeks heat with a light blush. *Samantha is single.* I can't help but feel a little bit giddy about that, especially since she looks so damn good. And Mallory is clearly trying to set us up. I think. I think I'm reading this correctly. And I'm on the same page as Mallory, I agree that Samantha deserves to be loved, I'm just not sure if Samantha is reading the same book as us.

"You ambushed her," I tell Mallory. "With me. Right?"

"Right," Mallory says, grinning. "It's a love ambush."

"Mallory..." I say, taking in a deep breath and then letting it slowly out. "I'm not sure Samantha, you know...likes me? We kind of left off on a rough patch, with me wanting to go to prom and making our relationship official and Samantha just...not wanting that. And then..."

"And then you left for school and our parents died and Sam closed herself off completely, focusing on me and Nelly," Mallory says. "It just wasn't the right time for a long-distance relationship, or any relationship, really. But maybe now is the right time to try again. It doesn't hurt to at least say hello."

"Have you been orchestrating this whole thing?" I ask. "Hiring me to teach art at the camp? Inviting us both to this party?"

"Hold up!" Mallory says, raising a single finger. "*You* contacted *me* about the job posting. I just took the opportunity of you coming back to town and ran with it. And Steve and I throw this party every year. It just happens to be the perfect occasion for you and Sam to get reacquainted. You're going to be living on the same mountain all summer. You're not going to be able to avoid each other for two whole months."

She's right. The town of Blytheton and the surrounding populated area are quite small. We're probably going to be running into each other at some point. I knew this would be a possibility when I applied for the job. I knew this was a possibility I *wanted* to happen. But now that it's happening, I am beyond nervous. But might as well take the rip-the-bandage-off approach and just go say hello to Samantha right now, right here, at this party. But my feet are glued to the spot.

"So..." Mallory says. "Are you going over, or should I drag Sam over here?"

"I'll...I'll go say hi myself, thank you," I say, and straighten my posture, heading over to Samantha with my chin held high.

It's been over a decade since high school, it would be petty of me to still hold a grudge about Samantha refusing to go to prom with me. I ended up going with a group of friends and we had a blast. But the closer I get to Samantha, the faster my heart beats. With every step fresh memories resurface: the tiny dimple she gets only in her left cheek when she smiles, the way her short strands of hair feel when I run my fingers through them, the way she smells like fresh, mountain air...

"Caroline," Samantha says as I finally reach her. She gives me a tight smile, one that isn't quite full enough to reveal her dimple, but just hearing her voice makes my heart flutter. But I tell my heart to simmer down.

"I'm here to teach art," I explain. "To the kids. At the camp. This camp. Here."

Well, those first few sentences went terribly. I want to find a shovel so I can start digging the hole I will reside in for the rest of my life.

Samantha nods. "That's great. How have you been?"

"Good. Good. Everything is good," I tell her, nodding and smiling like a complete fool. *Seriously, where can I find a shovel round here?*

"So, do you usually teach art? Is that your regular gig?" Samantha asks.

How is she being so calm and collected? Because she doesn't feel the same way I feel. That's why. She's moved on with her life, and I'm still reminiscing about the prom that could have been.

"Yes, I teach high school art in Providence," I say, and then congratulate myself on completing one whole normal sentence in the presence of Samantha. "And you? What do you do for a living?"

"I work for Mountain Rescue," Samantha says.

That makes sense. Samantha was always the outdoorsy type who wouldn't want a stifling office job. And then she nods and then I nod and then we're just two people, standing at a bustling party, nodding to each other.

Mallory swoops in, offering each of us a cupcake.

"Did you try Nelly's cupcakes yet?" Mallory asks.

"Yes," Samantha says, but still takes the dessert. Seems like she still has a sweet tooth.

"Isn't dinner soon?" I ask, but take the cupcake.

"Any minute now," Mallory says. "Why don't you two find a seat at one of the picnic tables?"

Chapter Three: Samantha

I manage to survive the dinner party, and by the end of the night things with Caroline feel a lot less awkward. But every time I look at Caroline, I have to suppress the butterflies that take flight in my stomach. It feels like I'm back in high school. I forgot about the way her eyes sparkle when she talks about her latest art projects. Tonight, she's been telling me about the classes she's planning to teach the kids at camp and she's positively glowing. I know nothing about art, but the joy and ease with which Caroline talks about it...I could listen to her talk all night. We're drinking hot chocolates and sitting in lawn chairs around a bonfire when she tells me about the videos she's posted on social media, some of which have gone viral.

"Really? What kind of videos?" I ask, genuinely curious.

I'll fully admit that sometimes, on late, quiet nights when I'm all alone (which is every night, really), I one hundred percent try to internet stalk her. But I never really find anything. She must be using something other than her real name. I've heard teachers often do that, so their students can't look them up. Or I figured she might have married and taken her spouse's last name. I had no idea she was posting art videos.

"The videos show my process," she explains. "You know how I like to use various objects to create texture and patterns and such—apparently people love it! I once used the texture on the bottom of a flip flop, bottle caps, bubble wrap, and old candy wrappers while painting a coral reef, and the video got over ten thousand views in the first two hours! It was wild!"

I definitely remember her obsession with using odd objects while painting. She'd create amazingly realistic paintings of majestic animals, but she always enjoyed the use of extra bits and pieces. She used to have boxes of random stuff in her bedroom, just for her painting projects.

"Ten thousand views? Really?" I ask. "I want to see that. Where can I watch your videos?"

"My screen name is Bubble Wrap Girl," she says with a coy smile.

"And you don't mind if I check it out?" I ask.

"Of course not," she says. But then her face falls, and I worry I've said something wrong.

"Everything okay?" I ask.

"Yeah...I just..." she trails off, and it looks like she's going to cry. She takes a deep breath and then finally says: "I haven't posted anything in over a year. My last ex threw out my boxes of art stuff, like the bubble wrap and fake plants and empty makeup containers. All that stuff. We were living together, and we kind of had a bad breakup. She threw all that stuff away before I had a chance to pack it up myself. She called them trash and said she'd been dying to get rid of them since the day I moved in with her. She said I wasn't a real artist. She said I was just a high school teacher and an internet fad. She said...well, she said a lot of things."

"I'm so sorry," I say. "That's horrible."

How could you date someone, live with someone, and not understand what was important to them? Throwing away Caroline's boxes of art supplies was just cruel. Caroline's parents used to jokingly complain about her 'boxes of garbage' when she lived at home, but they were just teasing her. They knew to never toss any of her stuff and they're the ones who encouraged her to get out of Blytheton and go to a good art college.

"Yeah, well, it was over a year ago," Caroline says, staring down into her mug of hot chocolate. "I feel...I feel like I'm over her, but I haven't been able to make any new videos. I haven't even started a new junk collection. I'm kind of hoping that getting away from the city and being in a new environment might help kick-start things. I won't have to think about *her* every time I pass by our favorite coffee shop, or second guess my art every time I try to pick up a paintbrush."

I've never had a serious relationship, so I don't know what it's like to go through a bad breakup. I felt broken when I refused to go to prom with Caroline and she stopped talking to me, but then my parents were gone, and I had bigger problems. Breakups definitely suck, but breaking up with a partner who'd throw out your belongings goes beyond awful. I want to find Caroline's ex-girlfriend and punch her in the face. My grip tightens on my mug just thinking about it, and I've never even punched anyone before. I've never *wanted* to punch anyone before. But hearing what Caroline went through...It lights a fire in me, one that wants to do nothing but protect Caroline from now on. I also want to do something to brighten her mood. She's still looking down and looking like she's fighting back tears, and I have no idea what to say. I can't find the words, but I see something that sparks an idea. I spot a small pinecone on the ground and pick it up.

"Here," I say, offering her the pinecone.

"What?" she asks, her green eyes gone wide.

"To start your new collection," I explain. "Didn't you used to have some pinecones in those boxes?"

"I did," she says. She takes the pinecone from me, her fingers lightly brushing mine as she does so. "Thank you, Sam."

It was just a small touch, but it makes me feel as light as air.

"And you are most definitely a real artist," I tell her. "Anyone who thinks otherwise is an idiot."

She scoffs, her delicate fingers wrapping tightly around the pinecone, while her other hand grips her mug, resting in her lap.

"I mean it," I say. "I've kept every single piece of artwork you've ever given me. Doodles from class and sketches and the painting of the wolf you made for me for my seventeenth birthday. Everything."

"You did not!" she says, a smile tugging at her lips.

"I did," I say. Of course I did. I've never been able to bring myself to pack any of it up. Not only did I keep it, but most of it is still pinned on the corkboard in my bedroom that I've had since I was a teen. Some of the more polished pieces, like her paintings, I've framed and hung up around my cabin, which I suddenly feel self-conscious about. I never expected her to be back to see it. *Is it weird that I kept everything?*

"That's sweet," Caroline says quietly, and turns away from me to watch the flames of the fire. The firelight dances on her cheeks and I swear they're a little bit pink. It could be the heat, but it could also be a blush.

We sit in comfortable silence as the fire dies down. People have been getting up and exiting the party for the past half hour, leaving in vehicles or going to their staff bunks. But I haven't been able to tear myself away, even though I'm getting tired and have an early shift in the morning. I just can't pull myself away from Caroline. Not for the first time in my life, I deeply regret how things ended with us.

"So...Looks like people are starting to leave. I guess this is good night?" Caroline says.

"I could walk you home?" I suggest, because I am so not ready to say goodnight.

My heart leaps for joy when she nods and smiles.

"I'd like that," Caroline says.

She leads the way, since I'm not sure which staff bunk she's in. Mallory and Steve have been working all spring on freshening up the bunks for campers and staff, and everything looks beyond amazing. Every single cabin is painted a vibrant color. Caroline leads me to a particularly bright magenta cabin with a yellow door.

"This is me," she says.

But instead of going inside, she lingers on the doorstep, fiddling with her keys. I tentatively reach out, touching her elbow. I hear her sudden inhale, and she looks up at me. I'm at least five inches taller than her, and I would just need to lower my head a tiny bit so my lips could meet hers...

"Samantha...?" she says, her eyes glancing at my lips.

"Hmm?" I ask.

"I missed you," she says softly.

"I missed you, too," I say, my voice just as soft.

And then she's rising on her tiptoes so she can kiss me. It's tentative and soft, exploring and cautious. Her hands rest on my shoulders as mine circle her slender waist, pulling her in closer. The sweet smell and taste of her strawberry lip gloss floods my memory with the kisses we shared as teens. After all these years, she still wears the same brand of lip gloss.

I've heard your sense of smell is the strongest link to memory and emotions, and I believe it. I feel like we've fallen back through time, the past decade and a half completely melting away as her lips part, letting me in, deepening our kiss. As my tongue slides against hers, she moans, pushing her body against mine.

But then she breaks our kiss, taking a step back.

"I'm sorry, I shouldn't have," she says hurriedly.

"I definitely wanted to kiss you," I say, and can't help the grin that spreads across my lips.

She bites her lip, fighting back a smile.

"Yeah?" she asks.

"Yeah," I say, pulling her into another kiss.

But she pulls away again.

"We shouldn't be doing this," she says, her voice barely a whisper.

"Why not?" I ask.

"Because I'm only here for two months and last time..."

And last time she left, and it broke my heart, but I don't say that out loud.

"How would you feel about a summer fling?" she suggests, her eyes sparkling. "Just you know...sex? And then I go back to Providence, and you stay here..."

I swallow the nervous lump in my throat. She's so fucking gorgeous. *I want to taste her.*

"Would I like to spend my summer fucking a beautiful woman?" I ask, my voice low as I trail kisses down her neck. "Why yes, I can't think of a better way to spend my summer."

Because why would I say no to that? I'd rather have two whole months of absolute bliss than nothing at all.

She gives me a mischievous grin before unlocking the door and pulling me in. The staff quarters has *three* bunk beds, and I stop in my tracks.

"Uh...do you have five roommates?" I ask quietly.

"Yes, but only one has arrived at camp so far, and she's still outside," Caroline says. She grabs the collar of my shirt and pulls me into the room and into a kiss. I kick the door shut behind us.

Even as we kiss, I feel her hands get to work, undoing all of my shirt's buttons. I caress her soft shoulders, pushing the thin straps of her sundress down, before reaching behind her for the zipper. She breaks the kiss and does a little shake, letting the blue dress pool around her feet. She's wearing a white lace bra and matching underwear set. She has sumptuous breasts, with a narrow waist and full, generous hips.

"For fuck's sake...your beautiful," I tell her.

I run my hands over her shoulders, along her sides, and over her hips, before reaching around to grab handfuls of her perky ass. She moans and steps closer, pressing her body against mine. I sink my hand down her front, cupping her pussy through her underwear and feeling her damp heat. She grinds into my hand, silently asking for more.

I bite at her earlobe and then ask: "Which is your bed?"

"The one at the back, bottom bunk," she says.

I cup her ass in my hands and scoop her up. She laughs and throws her arms and legs around me.

"*Shhhh!*" I hush her, even though I'm laughing, too. I feel like I'm a teenager again, fooling around in my bedroom while my parents have gone out, but my sisters are watching TV downstairs.

I set Caroline down on the bed, mindful not to bump her head on the top bunk, and then kneel before her. She sinks her fingers into my short hair, running her fingertips along my scalp, making me shiver.

"I missed you..." she says.

"But we haven't even gotten to the good part yet," I tease. I hold her gaze as I push her knees apart, then run my palms up the sides of her warm, luscious legs until I can hook my fingers under the thin straps of her bikini-cut underwear. She leans back on her elbows, thrusting her pussy forward, her lips slightly parted.

"Rip them off," she says breathily.

My fingers are tucked under the straps, but I lightly graze the lacey front with my thumbs.

"But they look expensive..." I tease.

She grinds forward again, and I can smell her arousal. My pussy throbs as her scent fills the air.

"Rip. Them. Off," she demands.

I tug at the thin straps. She gasps as the fabric snaps free and then I tug the underwear completely off, tossing them onto the floor. Her pink pussy glistens before me, inviting and sexy as fuck. I don't waste time. My hands grip her inner thighs as I bend down and run my tongue up her slit, getting my first taste of her warm pussy. She's just as delicious as I remember.

"Fuck yes..." she moans, and then she hurriedly removes her bra.

I take a moment to worship her perfect cleavage, filling my mouth with one of her tightened nipples as my hand massages her other breast. She arches into my touch, moaning appreciatively. I switch breasts, giving her other nipple a light bite, but I need to taste more of her pussy.

I make my way back down, between her legs. I nibble and lick her pussy, eliciting a sensual groan of pleasure from her. I keep my mouth on her clit, but sink two fingers into her, and she gasps. She grinds into my fingers and mouth, moaning every time I thrust my fingers into her. Her cries become quicker, louder, more feral. I keep fucking her with my fingers, but I remove my mouth so I can take a moment to reprimand her.

"The whole camp can hear you," I tease.

"Fuck. Sorry," she says.

"It's fucking hot," I say, and then dive back in, my mouth latching onto her pussy.

She moans, quieter now, sounding frustrated she can't be too loud.

"More...fuck me more..." she says.

I push a third finger in and her breath hitches, but I can tell she isn't quite there yet, she just likes the feeling of being nice and full. I keep going, pounding into her pussy with my fingers while mercilessly working her clit with my tongue. I can hear her breath coming in clipped, quick gasps and then I feel the clench of her pussy around my fingers as she comes. She lets out one last gasp of absolute pleasure before collapsing on the bed, breathing heavily.

"Fuck yes..." she moans, but then she's pushing herself back up. "Come here," she says, tugging me closer by my shirt collar again. She's smiling brightly, full of afterglow from her orgasm, and she's never looked more beautiful, her red hair messy, her pale, freckled face flushed pink. "Your turn."

Still kneeling before her, she wraps me in her legs. She shoves her hand down my jeans, while her other hand tugs at my buttons and then unzips my fly, giving herself more freedom of movement. I moan appreciatively as her fingers find my slick pussy. I capture her mouth in a kiss and rock into her touch, but she pulls away.

"You are fucking soaked, Sam," she says.

"Mmmmm," I say, no longer able to form words.

There's a burst of laughter and it sounds like it's just outside our cabin. Her hand freezes, her fingers deep in my pussy. My whole body tenses, anticipating the door opening with Caroline naked and her hand down my pants.

"Fuck," I say, coming back to my senses. I grab her wrist and gently tug her hand away from me.

"It's good, it's fine, they've moved on," she says hurriedly between kisses. She tries to touch me again, but I push her away.

"Fuck, this is your new job," I tell her. "You're a camp teacher. We shouldn't have..."

"It's not like any of the kids are here yet," she protests.

We hear nearby laughter again and we both tense up. I stand, doing my pants back up before buttoning my shirt. But Caroline is still sitting on the edge of the bed, naked and pouting.

"Put your clothes on," I tell her, my voice stern.

She bites her lip and runs her foot up the side of my leg. "I like when you're bossy, Sam."

"Put your clothes on," I repeat.

She sighs and reaches over to the little dresser next to her bed, pulling out some pink cotton pajamas. She holds my gaze the entire time and then stands before me, dressed and ready for bed.

"Good girl," I tell her and give her a pat on the ass.

She looks up at me with big green eyes, and then slaps her hand across my still-aching pussy and squeezes me through my jeans. I bite back a gasp, wanting so much more, but knowing we should never have started any of this, in this shared cabin, at her brand new job.

"We're not done," Caroline says. "Next time I see you, your pussy is mine."

I narrow my eyes at her and grasp her forearms, but I'm smiling. "Excuse me? Just a moment ago, I was the dominant one."

She just shrugs, shaking off my light grasp. "We'll see about that."

Chapter Four: Caroline

I don't realize just how nervous I am to run art classes for a group of young kids until I step foot in the art cabin, trailing behind Mallory. Teenagers I'm used to. But grade school kids? Kids who are staying at a sleep-away camp? It's an entirely different dynamic.

"We tried to get you everything you might need, but feel free to poke around and let us know if you'd like anything else," Mallory says. "Mrs. Clements, the widow who lives in the giant mansion on the mountain, do you remember her? She's been amazing with her generous donations, plus it's our record-breaking year for camp enrollment, so ask away! You need more acrylic paints, more brushes, more sketch pads—just let me or Steve know, and we'll hook you up."

"That's amazing, thank you," I say, already in awe of the number of supplies in the room.

And it's good stuff, not just cheap dollar store fare. But maybe I should collect a box of oddities, too. My hand sinks into the pocket of my denim overall shorts and closes around the tiny pinecone Samantha gave to me at the campfire. I haven't had the courage to start a new box of oddities since my evil ex trashed my last one, but maybe I could have a box for the kids to add to.

"You'll have at least one of the teen camp counselors in class with you at all times, as your teacher's assistant," Mallory continues. "But this isn't school, it's camp. The kids who come to your classroom will be kids who actually want to create something. And you can have ideas for lessons, but we kind of like letting the kids be free while they're here. For a lot of them, this is their safe haven; a place to exist with other people like them and people who acknowledge them for who they truly are. A place where they can be themselves."

"That's amazing, by the way," I tell her. "The fact that this camp caters to LGBTQ+ kids is just...amazing. Thank you, and Steve, for doing this."

I knew pretty early on that I liked girls, and when I first talked about it with my parents, they were amazing, but I know many people don't have that kind of experience. I feel incredibly thankful for Mallory and Steve and this camp, and the opportunity to be a part of it.

"Well, I'm pansexual and married to a trans man, my older sister is a lesbian, my younger sister is also pan, and both our parents considered themselves bi, so...it's the kind of place all of us would have liked to have when we were growing up, right?" Mallory says. "The camp my parents used to run was just a regular summer camp, but Steve and I wanted to do things a little bit differently. And while my parents were super open about this stuff, there are so many kids that don't have that, or kids who have parents who want to be supportive, but are still trying to figure out what they can do to help. And on one hand, Steve and I discussed how we didn't want this camp to feel like a place set apart from others, we want ourselves and these kids to feel included in the world, but on the other hand...sometimes it's nice to have a space that feels truly safe, especially when you're young and still figuring everything out. And of course, kids and staff don't have to openly identify as LGBTQ+, but we obviously make it clear we have a focus on that."

"It's definitely a balancing act," I agree. "To seek out the comfort of our own communities, but to also just want to be accepted for who we are, anywhere and everywhere."

"We do have a robust team of social workers on staff," Mallory says. "If a camper ever opens up to you and you feel overwhelmed, you can guide them to one of the social workers. You're also welcome to speak to a social worker for guidance if the camper only wants to talk to you. And if you have any questions at all, you can always come talk to either me or Steve."

"Thank you," I tell her. "I am super excited to be here, and incredibly thankful for this opportunity."

"We're excited to have you," Mallory says. "So, I'll leave you to it. Take a look around and let us know if you need anything."

"Thanks!" I say again, and wave goodbye to Mallory.

I walk around the classroom, taking note of everything. It seems like Mallory and Steve really went overboard, making sure there are plenty of craft supplies, from fuzzy pipe cleaners to sophisticated sets of oil paints. For the time being, I don't think I need to ask for anything. I'll wait and see which direction the kids want to take things, and if there is an art project they're interested in that we don't have supplies for, I can inquire then. There was an on-line camp teacher course I had to take before starting, which basically recommended teachers just go with the flow, and that sounded just fine to me. There's also more training the rest of this week, before the campers arrive, but today

Mallory wanted us to settle in and get acquainted with the camp, our classrooms, and the surrounding area.

Many of the teachers and camp counselors will be coming from all across the country and some from abroad, and while I'm technically from out of town, this is also my homecoming. I know this place. These mountains and forests and the little town of Blytheton; everything feels cozy and familiar. I was barely in the town of Blytheton when I first arrived, just long enough to see the main strip looked pretty much the same, but then I was catching a ride up the mountain to the campground. I really hope I get an opportunity to visit the town sometime this summer, but I don't have a car of my own, so I'll have to rely on the kindness of others letting me tag along.

One of my favorite things to do when I was younger was going on nature hikes with a sketchpad, and I'm eager to get reacquainted with the forest and trails of my youth. I select a small sketchpad and some pencils, along with a blanket from my bunk and my bottle of water I wear in a sling like a purse, and my bear spray, and I head off into the woods. I follow the hiking trail, but I used to walk off the beaten path all the time when I was a teen. It's been a while since I've been in these woods, but I already feel comfortable and like I've barely been away at all. I wander off the path, in search of a nice place to lay my blanket so I can sit down, sketch, listen to the birdsong, and just forget...*everything*. This is why I came here: to get away from Providence, and to get away from reminders of my ex.

But there's one thing, one person, who keeps resurfacing, insisting I think about *her*: Samantha. And our kiss. How perfect it was. And how much more I want.

CHAPTER FIVE: SAMANTHA

I've just finished my shift with Mountain Rescue, and instead of driving straight home, I make a detour over to Camp Pride. Since I start early in the morning, I'm usually done around mid-afternoon. I tell myself I'm just checking in with Mallory and Steve, making sure everything is running smoothly, and I'll ask if they need me to pick up anything in town. I need to do a grocery run myself, so might as well ask if they need anything. Could I have just called and asked? Sure. But then I wouldn't have the opportunity to accidentally bump into Caroline again. My pussy throbs at the thought of being able to see her again, to taste her again...but I need to calm the fuck down. We tentatively agreed to a no-strings-attached-sex-summer, but that doesn't mean I can just show up to camp every single day to make out with her, especially once the campers arrive.

I walk into camp and find it bustling with new staff, but so far, I don't see Caroline's familiar head of vibrant red hair. I do find Steve, though. He's tall and slender, with short dark hair. He smiles warmly when he sees me and walks over.

"Hey Sam," Steve says. "What brings you back so soon?"

"I'm doing a grocery run into town," I explain. "You guys need anything?"

"Really? You'd be willing to pick some stuff up for us? Because somehow, we ended up forgetting to buy laundry detergent. If you could pick us up a couple of bottles to hold us over until our bulk order arrives, that would be awesome."

"Yeah, definitely," I say.

"Oh, and Caroline, the new art teacher, she mentioned at lunch that she wanted to go into town sometime and she doesn't have a car," Steve adds. "Maybe you could take her?"

"Um...yeah, sure," I say, and suddenly my heart is pounding so fast it's like I've just run up the mountain.

"I'll go let her know," Steve says, and jogs away.

Moments later, Steve returns with Caroline in tow. They're chatting amicably, but she stops mid-sentence when she sees me, a grin spreading across her freckled face.

"Oh..." she says. "Steve didn't mention it was *you*."

"Um..." Steve says, looking between the two of us. "Is there a problem?"

I'm not sure how much Steve knows about me and Caroline. He didn't grow up in the mountains—Mallory met him on a dating app, so he's from out of town and doesn't know all the old high school gossip.

"No, no problem here," Caroline says quickly, giving me a wink.

"Oh, this is new! And super cute!" Caroline says, stopping in front of Bliss Cupcakes & Café. "Can we go in before we get your groceries?"

"This is where Nelly works," I explain. "And sure, we can go in."

I open the door for her, and Caroline practically skips into the bakery. The walls have pink and white striped wallpaper, the floor is a checkerboard of pink and white tiles, and a great big pink chandelier hangs from the ceiling.

"Oh, wow…" Caroline says, taking everything in.

Caroline's always been a girly girl. She's currently wearing a pink blouse with a cute pair of denim overall shorts that have flowers embroidered all over them. Of course she loves this place.

"Hey!" Nelly says, peeking out from the back kitchen. She wipes her hands on her pink apron and walks out to greet us. "What brings you two here?"

She looks from me to Caroline, grinning and bouncing on her toes.

"This place is adorable," Caroline gushes. "This was not here back in the day, right?"

"No, it's only been here about five years," Nelly says. "My boss, Gwen, owns the place. It used to be a basic bread bakery, but Gwen gave it a makeover. So, what can I get you?"

"Which ones did you make?" Caroline asks, looking through the glass at the rows of baked goods: cupcakes, macaroons, and brownies with pink heart sprinkles.

"All of it," Nelly says, smiling proudly. "Gwen is off today."

"Well, I can never say no to chocolate," Caroline says. "I'll have a brownie, please."

"I'll have the same," I say, and take out my wallet.

I know two things are about to happen: first, Nelly is going to insist I get the 'family discount', which means she gives me stuff for free, and second, Caroline is going to insist she pay for her own brownie.

I'm not going to let either of those things happen. I pull out a twenty-dollar bill and put it on the pink linoleum counter, shoving it over to Nelly.

"Not. A. Word," I tell her in my best stern-big-sister voice.

Nelly frowns. "Fine. But do you want your change?"

Caroline is fiddling in her purse for her own wallet. "How much is mine?"

"The twenty covers both," I say, still using my big sister voice. "And you can keep the change, Nelly."

"*Samantha*," Nelly whines.

"Just take it," I tell her.

She shakes her head, but takes the twenty and rings us through, dumping the change into the mason jar for tips.

"Thank you," I say.

Nelly gives each of us our brownies in a pink paper bag and we make our way to the bench outside the bakery.

"Thank you," Caroline says. "For the ride. And the brownie."

"You're welcome," I say.

"But just because you took me into town and bought me a baked good at an adorable bakery, it doesn't mean we're on a date," Caroline says. "We're not dating this summer we're just...doing other stuff. The kind of stuff that has no strings attached."

"Of course," I say, biting into my heavenly brownie. "After this, I'm getting groceries and picking up laundry detergent for Steve. Those would be some pretty weird date activities."

"It would," she agrees, and takes a bite of her own brownie. And then her eyes go wide as she finishes chewing. "Oh. My. God."

"My sister has a gift," I agree, and polish off my brownie, Caroline making quick work of her own.

"Can I have a dozen more?" she asks.

"Sure," I say, jumping to my feet. Before she can stop me, I walk briskly into the bakery and get two more brownies.

"I wasn't serious!" Caroline says as I present her with her new brownie bag.

"We'll save them for later," I tell her. "They'll be our dessert."

"Oh, really?" Caroline asks. "And what's for dinner?"

"That depends. What do you want?" I ask.

I'm walking down the quaint street to the grocery store, Caroline walking at my side. This doesn't really feel like a date, but somehow going grocery shopping, and if she allows it, picking out a dinner together and going home to cook it, feels so much more familiar and domestic than a date. My stride is confident, and I'm really hoping she goes along with my suggestion of dinner, but I'm also incredibly nervous she's going to turn me down because it's crossing some sort of no-dating-just-sex line.

"As friends," I amend, since she still hasn't said anything. "I just want to catch up more, that's all."

"That's all," she says sternly. "And I wouldn't say no to a pasta dish?"

"I can do pasta," I say, and open the grocery store door for her.

CHAPTER SIX: CAROLINE

Even though my common sense is saying: *don't eat dinner with the gorgeous woman you want to have sex with all summer*, I...go and eat dinner with the gorgeous woman I want to have sex with all summer. I don't entirely know what I was picturing when I made the offer, but I didn't intend to do anything that resembled a relationship. I just pictured fucking. Lots and lots of fucking. Mostly at her place, since doing it in my bunk was pretty risqué and not professional in the least. But we just went grocery shopping together and now we're going to cook and eat dinner together. That doesn't seem very casual to me.

I follow Samantha inside her rustic mountain home, the same house she grew up in, and I'm flooded with nostalgia. Being on the main strip of Blytheton today was surreal. Even though a lot had changed, like the addition of the adorable bakery, other things, like the grocery store, hadn't changed much at all. The same is true for Samantha's house: it's nearly identical to when we were growing up. Since her family lived so much farther up the mountain, and my parents lived in the quaint suburbs closer to town, if I spent time at Samantha's, it was usually a prolonged amount of time, such as a sleepover. Some of which got a little bit...*steamy*. I feel a gentle, eager pulse in my pussy, thinking about being horny teenagers, exploring each other's bodies, being each other's first. God, I want to climb Samantha, the tall and sturdy mountain woman, and make her mine. I still owe her a good fucking after what she did to me in my bunk.

"You can go relax, maybe find something for us to watch on TV while I get dinner ready," Samantha says, snapping me out of my dirty thoughts about her wet pussy. "I'm just going to whip up some simple pasta. It won't be long."

"I can help," I offer.

"Nah, it's fine," she says. "Go make yourself at home."

A pink blush climbs up her cheeks and Samantha scratches her neck.

"I mean, you've been here before and..." she mumbles. "You remember your way around? Not much has changed."

I give her a smile. "I remember my way around."

I make my way to the rec room, down the hall from the kitchen. Samantha wasn't kidding when she said she hadn't changed much. It's the same navy blue couch with the blue quilted pillows her mom made. There is one new addition: the wolf painting I did for Samantha is framed and hanging on the wall above the couch. She wasn't kidding. She really does have my old artwork up. A warmth spreads through my limbs, and I hug my arms around myself.

I always felt guilty about not being here for Samantha when she lost both her parents, but my parents would have been furious if I decided at the last minute not to go to the Rhode Island School of Design, especially since I had been offered a full scholarship. Besides, we weren't really talking when it happened, because of the whole prom thing. I remind myself that's in the past. I can't change what happened between me and Samantha.

I turn on the TV and start scrolling through Samantha's streaming choices. I purposely ignore anything that looks remotely romantic and end up picking a movie that looks like a creepy murder mystery. I would bet good money that no one is going to fall in love in this movie. But just to be sure, I take out my phone and double check. Yep. I confirm this is a 'safe' movie for a pair of super casual friends-with-benefits to watch together.

The pasta and brownies have been eaten, the movie is over, and my feet somehow ended up in Samantha's lap. She's been giving me a glorious foot massage for the last half hour of the movie. It's something she always used to do during movies and it kind of just...*happened*. And she's amazing at it. No one has ever given me a foot massage since Samantha. None of my exes ever offered. The movie credits are rolling by, and I watch as her strong hands massage every single perfect place in my feet. I feel her eyes on me, and I look up.

"What?" I ask.

"You know we don't have to..." she trails off.

"Have to what?" I tease, knowing exactly what she's alluding to.

"We don't have to carry on with what we proposed the other night," she says, the foot massage coming to an end. I pull my feet back, tucking them under myself.

"You don't want to?" I ask, my heart sinking. All I've been thinking about the entire evening is going down on Samantha, getting reacquainted with her pussy, and making her come on my tongue at least once, maybe twice.

"I want to...I just..." she says, running a hand through her short hair.

"I owe you," I remind her. "You got to taste me, but I haven't been able to taste you again."

Samantha swallows and lets out a long breath.

"Fuck me..." she grumbles.

"That's the plan, yes," I say sweetly, knowing she likes to receive just as much as give, and I'm the same way.

I sit up on my knees and then prowl over to her side of the couch. She parts her legs for me, welcoming me into her warmth.

"Mmmhmm?" I hum, my fingers going to her fly, popping the button open and dragging down the zip. She gives me the nod to go ahead. I tug at her jeans, and she lifts her ass, allowing me to pull them all the way off, her socks being dragged off along with them. And then, with her help, I make quick work of her underwear. I graze a knuckle along her pussy lips, teasing her.

"Everything off," I say, leaving her pussy behind so I can help her with the buttons of her shirt. She's wearing a plain gray cotton sports bra underneath, the same type of bra she's always worn. The same type of bra that is always a pain in the ass to get off.

"Seriously?" I ask, tugging at the hem.

"Let me do it," she grumbles, and pulls it over her head.

I place a single finger on her lips, smiling. It's almost hard to believe I'm here, back in this house, with my Samantha. She holds perfectly still as I gently run my finger down her chin, her throat, her upper chest, and then between her small breasts. I reach over and give each a gentle squeeze, feeling her hardened nipples against my palm, and she moans appreciatively. But then I continue my single-finger descent down her toned abs.

"Fuck, Sam, you've been working out?" I ask.

She shrugs. "Maybe. What kind of a mountain woman would I be if I can't chop my own firewood and throw my woman over my shoulder when I want to fuck her?"

I laugh, tracing the faint outline of her abs. "Am I your woman?"

"Yes," she says, breathing the word.

I meet her eyes as my finger continues its quest, gliding over her pubis mound and her soft thatch of dark blonde hair, teasing her clit for a moment, before sinking into her pussy and feeling how deliciously wet she is. She breaks our gaze as she throws her head back and moans softly. I move back to her clit with her wetness on my finger, circling and applying pressure the way I remember she likes it, teasing more pleasure from her.

But then she snaps her head back up, her gaze heated. "Take your clothes off."

"But then I'll have to stop touching you," I pout.

"Take your clothes off," she says. "I want to see you."

I nod and unclip the top of my overalls before unbuttoning my blouse and peeling it off. Sam licks her lips, her eyes on my heavy-feeling breasts. I purposely wore another one of my pretty, lacy bras that pushes my breasts up and makes them look huge. I know my sexy mountain woman likes my tits.

"Touch yourself," I tell her. She isn't the only one who likes to be bossy while they fuck.

She narrows her eyes and doesn't follow my command.

"Touch yourself while I undress," I say. "But don't make yourself come."

She sighs and reaches down, slowly touching her clit.

"That's it," I tell her. "Sink your finger in, feel how wet you are."

She does as I tell her and watching her is fucking hot. I feel my skin warm and my pussy aches. I reach around and unclasp my bra. I shrug it off, freeing my breasts. Samantha moans appreciatively, her eyes on my chest. She bites her lip and rubs herself harder.

"You like them?" I ask playfully, my hands squeezing my breasts, pushing them together.

Samantha nods, but then says, "Your overalls. Take off your fucking overalls."

I stand up and *slowly* start to shimmy out of my cute little overall shorts.

"Fuck...Caroline..." Samantha moans. "Hurry the fuck up."

I let the overalls fall to the ground, revealing my pink lacy underwear. I kick my overalls off my ankles, and then sink a finger under the lacy fabric of my underwear, touching my clit. I close my eyes, enjoying the sensation before dipping into my pussy and feeling how wet I am.

"Off. Now," Samantha demands.

I pull the underwear down and step out of them, standing naked in front of Samantha's hungry gaze. The way she looks at me makes me feel beautiful, sexy, and *wanted*.

"Make yourself come," she says, her voice barely a whisper.

"Are you going to, too?" I ask.

She nods.

"You're going to watch me fuck myself?" I ask.

She nods again.

My legs tremble as I rub my clit harder, my eyes locked on hers. I can see in my peripheral vision the movements of her hand on her pussy, vigorously fucking herself.

"But are you still going to let me fuck you?" I ask.

She nods. "Finger yourself."

I widen my stance and slip my fingers in, watching Samantha as she watches me. I don't think I've ever fucked myself so thoroughly while standing. My legs are beginning to feel like jelly, so I climb back onto the couch, my wet fingers never leaving my clit. I lay back, our legs and pussies facing each other.

"You're so fucking beautiful…" Samantha says.

"You too, babe," I say and feel the euphoric feeling of my building orgasm. "I'm…I'm almost there. Are you?"

"Fuck. Yes."

"Now," I pant, unable to ride it out much longer, desperate to let myself come. "Please. Now."

"Now," she agrees.

I cry out as I feel my orgasm violently ripple through me, followed by a soft, pulsing ache in my core. Samantha moans, throwing her head back as her fingers slow. My chest heaves as I catch my breath and slowly come back down, but I still feel hungry for more.

"Come here," Samantha says. She reaches over and grabs me by the wrist, tugging me back to her. I rearrange myself and playfully fall into her naked lap.

I'm at just the right place to kiss her mouth. She cradles my head, deepening our kiss.

"Ride my thigh," she whispers into our kiss.

Without fully parting our lips, we rearrange ourselves, so Samantha is fully propped up on the armrest, one bare leg stretched out on the couch, the other dangling off the side, making room for me to climb onto her thigh. I spread myself over her leg and then sink down, rubbing my pussy on her warm skin, hands gripping her shoulders.

"You are so fucking wet," Samantha moans.

I reach down and stroke Samantha's clit, eliciting a shiver.

"Do you want me to come on your thigh while I fuck your pussy?" I whisper into her ear.

"Mmm...yes," she says. She lays back against the armrest as I sink two fingers in, my thumb taking care of her clit. Her body pushes into my hand, causing her thigh to undulate beneath me and rubbing my pussy just right. I angle myself so every thrust against her thigh hits my tender clit.

"Fuck...I'm..." I gasp. I'm so turned on by Samantha's toned body, the feel of her wet pussy on my hand and her strong, warm thigh beneath me, that it isn't going to take much to get me off. "I'm not going to...last very long..." I tell her.

"Let go, baby," she says. "I'm right there with you."

I gasp as my orgasm rocks through me, and Samantha lets out a cry of her own. I feel her pussy pulse around my fingers, and I dive in for another long, sensuous, satisfying kiss. Slowly, we come back down from our high together. I wrap my arms around her shoulders, laying my head on her chest. I can hear her rapidly beating heart and I can feel mine beating just as fast.

"Sam..." I say. "That was..."

"Incredible?" she asks quietly.

"Yeah, incredible. Were we this good in high school?" I ask with a laugh.

"Yes," she says with a laugh of her own.

I think back to all of our frenzied, passionate, first-love lovemaking of our youth and yes, things were pretty fucking hot back then, too. Not a single woman I've been with since Samantha has ever compared to *her*. I used to think it was just because she was my first: my first sexual partner and my first love. Maybe that *is* it. Maybe that's why I feel such a deeper connection with her. Maybe it's why I feel more self-confident, and sexier and more beautiful and more turned on, when Samantha and I make love, than with any other woman. And maybe *that's* it. Maybe because when I'm with Samantha, my mindset is completely different and I feel like we're making love to each other, connecting on a whole other level, and not just fucking each other senseless. I mean...we do fuck each other senseless, but...there's more.

But *fuck*. There wasn't supposed to be more. It was *supposed* to be just fucking, not lovemaking. It probably should have been obvious to me the moment I laid eyes on her at the party, but I'm just coming to my senses now: I'm one-hundred percent still in love with Samantha.

Chapter Seven: Samantha

My heart is beating like crazy, and it's not just because of the mind-blowing sex I just had with Caroline. It's because I missed her and I never want her to leave, ever again. Or I need to go with her to Rhode Island. Or meet somewhere in the middle. I don't care. I just know she's the one for me and this stupid sex-with-no-strings-attached-summer is already falling to pieces, and it's only been two sexual episodes and barely one week. We're both idiots. Beautiful, lovesick idiots.

"Stay the night?" I ask, hugging Caroline tighter.

"Sam..." Caroline says.

She pushes herself up, and I release her. And then she's scooping her clothes off the floor and pulling her underwear back on.

"What are you doing?" I ask, but I reach for my shirt, wrapping it around my shoulders and doing the buttons back up.

"I should go," Caroline says. "I don't think it's a good idea if I stay the night."

I glance outside, into the pitch darkness, and Caroline follows where I look.

"Shit, I forgot how dark it gets out here," she says, pulling her blouse on.

I grab my phone from the coffee table to check the time.

"It's one in the morning," I say. "Do camp staff have a curfew?"

Caroline pauses. "We're technically supposed to be in our bunks before midnight, but we're adults, so Mallory and Steve don't *really* enforce those rules."

"But you'd potentially be waking everyone up if you stumble in at two in the morning," I say, desperately wanting her to stay, but she still looks hesitant. "You can stay in the guestroom."

"You have a guest room?" she asks.

"It's technically Mallory's old room," I explain. "Unlike Nelly, she actually cleared all her stuff out after she got married. So, it's just a room with a bed that doesn't really belong to anyone, therefore, it's the guest room."

Caroline nods slowly, clearly liking the option of not having to ask me to drive her all the way back to camp and sneak into her bunk, but she also doesn't have to sleep next to me, like a real couple would.

"Okay," she says, coming to a final decision. "I'll stay in the guest room."

I toss and turn all night, knowing Caroline is sound asleep on the other side of my bedroom wall. Falling back in love with her was too easy, especially when we're intimate together. But she clearly only wants a summer of hot sex and nothing else, or she would have come and slept in my bed, curled up against me as my little spoon.

I have an early morning Mountain Rescue shift tomorrow, as usual, so I'm desperate to fall asleep. I try to put her out of my mind and not think about her tongue lapping mine, or the way her hot pussy feels against my thigh, or the way she tasted the other night...

Good god, I feel like I've become a horny teenager again. I haven't been with many women since Caroline, and it's been like...over a year since the last time I had any kind of sex, so it's no wonder I'm hyper fixated on the hot sex we just had on my couch, but I really need to fall asleep.

I eventually sleep, but when I wake next, it feels like I barely slept a wink, and my alarm is going off. I sit up, feeling groggy and running a hand through my mussed-up hair. And...*do I smell coffee? And pancakes?*

I make my way downstairs and find Caroline in the kitchen, wearing nothing but one of my plaid shirts that falls mid-thigh on her. Her face is fresh and clean, not a speck of makeup, which makes her look considerably younger. And beautiful. She gives me a wide smile as she notices me and then quickly flips a pancake.

"Good morning," she says.

"Um...good morning?" I answer groggily.

"How did you sleep?" she asks.

"I...feel like I didn't," I answer. "How about you?"

"Oh, I usually completely pass out not long after orgasming so...I slept really well," she says.

The way she mentions our sex so casually...I decide not to dwell on it.

"Why are you up so early? And making breakfast in my kitchen?" I ask.

"Because I know you start your Mountain Rescue shifts at an insanely early hour and you need to drive me back to camp before you start," she says. "If you don't mind? I could maybe call Steve or Mallory, but then I'd have to explain—"

"No, I'll drive you," I quickly cut in, not wanting to deal with Mallory's gloating just yet.

"And I thought making pancakes would be a good way to thank you, for driving me," she explains, removing her current pancake from the frying pan and adding it to a stack she's keeping warm in the oven. "Also, everything is exactly where it's always been, so it wasn't that hard to wake up and make us breakfast."

"Where did you find that shirt?" I ask, unable to resist eyeing her smooth, naked legs, and her bare feet with her pink painted toenails.

"Laundry room," she says. "You had a fresh load waiting to be folded, so I helped myself. Do you mind?"

"No, I don't mind," I tell her. Because I can't get over how damn sexy she looks wearing nothing but one of my shirts.

I want to walk up to her, wrap her in my arms, and hug her from behind while she makes us breakfast. I want this: her, in my home. Our home. *Always.* I am so fucking screwed. Instead of hugging her, I grab the pot of coffee she's already brewed and pour myself a cup. I see she's already made her own, sitting on the counter within her reach while she makes the pancakes.

I grab plates, utensils, and maple syrup, and bring everything to the table. She finishes cooking the last pancake and we sit down to eat. The pancakes are delicious and fluffy, and she's added in cinnamon and chocolate chips, just the way I like it.

"Thank you," I say. "They're delicious."

"You're welcome," she says, tucking into her own stack.

Yeah...the no strings attached thing was a very, very bad idea.

CHAPTER EIGHT: CAROLINE

"Stop the truck," I say.

We're halfway back to camp, and Samantha has to get to work, but I need her to stop driving. She slowly rolls to a stop and pulls over as much as possible on the tree-lined road.

"Are you okay?" Samantha asks, putting the truck in park and looking over at me.

I'm gripping the door handle, feeling nauseous. I'm not carsick I'm just...I can't stand the thought of continuing this facade of a sex romp summer.

"I can't do this," I say, shaking my head slowly. "I just can't..."

"What? Teach at the camp?" Samantha asks. "You're an art teacher by trade, of course you can do this. The kids are a bit younger and it's at summer camp but—"

"No, not my new job," I say. "This. Us."

"Us?" she asks quietly.

"I'm sorry, I don't think I can keep up a physical relationship with you," I tell her, finally finding the courage to look her in the eye. "I can't do this."

"Why...can't you do this?" she asks, her brow furrowed. "I'm pretty sure last night confirmed we're pretty damn good at it."

I laugh, and then: "Because I already want more."

"More sex?" Samantha asks. "Because you look sexy as hell right now, we could maybe have a roadside quickie, but I do need to get to work—"

"No!" I say, feeling frustrated and balling my hands into fists. "Why are you being so...so dense?"

"Dense?" Her eyes go wide, and she's looking at me like I've gone crazy.

I take a deep breath and *look* at her: really, really look at her. My Samantha. The very first person I ever gave my heart to. And the very last person I want to give it to.

"Because I love you," I tell her, my voice hushed as if saying it as quietly as possible will make it less of a big deal if she turns me down.

She's silent. She breaks our gaze and looks out the window, away from me.

"Samantha?" I say, just as quiet as before.

She finally looks back at me.

"You're only here for the summer," she says. "And then you're going to leave. You're going to leave me. Again."

"What if I stayed?" I suggest. "My whole life, before I left: I always thought my life was somewhere out there, at university, in another state, anywhere but here. And then the entire time I've been gone, all I can think about is whether or not I should have left. If I should have left Blytheton, if I should have left you...But the thought of coming back here, coming back to you, and finding things and people and you...Possibly finding out that you have moved on without me, was too hard to bear. I never tried looking you up online. I didn't want to know if you were single or married or whatever. But then...I saw the job listing for Camp Pride and it felt like the right time to come home, like it was meant to be. And I already feel like I'm home. Every second I spend with you; I feel like I've truly found my home and the place I'm meant to be."

"Caroline..." Samantha says, reaching out to clasp my hand in hers.

"I'm sorry if you don't feel the same. I'm sorry if I'm moving too fast," I say, my lower lip trembling and my eyes brimming with tears. "But I can't keep having mindless, amazing, mind-blowing sex with you if this is how I feel, and you don't feel the same."

"But I do feel the same," Samantha says. "I love you. I want you to stay. And I feel it, too. You, Caroline, are my home, *my everything*."

Well, that opens the floodgates. Tears run down my face, and I sniffle: *she feels the same!*

"I love you!" I say again, just because I can, just because I know when I say those three words, they're one-hundred percent reciprocated.

"I love you," Samantha says and pulls me into a kiss.

But then she breaks off our kiss and abruptly gets out of the truck.

"Samantha?" I call, as she rounds the hood and comes over to my door. She yanks it open and reaches over me, undoing my seatbelt. "What are you doing?"

"Maybe I didn't have time for a roadside quickie for my summer fling, but I definitely have time for a roadside quickie for my girlfriend," she says with a grin.

She grabs my thighs and spins me around, so my legs are facing her, dangling out the side of the truck. She reaches up and unclips my overalls and then yanks them down, pulling my underwear down with them. She pulls everything over my feet, my sandals falling off in the process. And then she pushes my knees apart.

"Samantha!" I cry out, feeling the morning mountain breeze on my bare, wet pussy.

"This is my route," she tells me. "I drive along here every morning. No one is ever around, so I'm going to eat your pussy at the side of the road. Okay?"

"Um...okay," I say, feeling the familiar swell of need building in my core.

"Good," she says, and then dives in, her tongue lapping at my entrance.

"Oh fuck..." I mumble, one hand on the dash, the other gripping the edge of my seat.

She fucks me with her tongue, and I push my pussy into her face, wanting more of everything. She reaches up, her palm spread on my stomach, her thumb gently rubbing my clit.

"Fuck...fuck ...fuck..." I mumble as the first wave of my orgasm flows through me.

She fucks me over the edge and back, gently slowing her motions. And then she places one small, chaste kiss on my spent pussy before standing up and kissing me on the mouth, my own taste flooding my senses.

I snake my hand down her pants, caressing her wet pussy.

"I should really get to work..." she mumbles into our kiss.

"You're so worked up I can make you come hard and fast," I tease.

"You ain't wrong..." she says, and I can feel her smile against my lips.

I know from past experience my girl can get off nice and fast with just some clit teasing if she's already worked herself into a frenzy, and I'm pretty sure eating me out roadside is just the ticket to getting her thoroughly frenzied. I continue to firmly stroke her clit, and she braces herself with one arm on the frame of the truck. It's not long before her breath grows ragged and she moans, resting her forehead against mine as a shiver runs through her. She lets out a long sigh and takes a step back, straightening her clothes. She watches me with a sleepy, hooded, post-sex gaze, as I lick her nectar off my fingers.

"Fucking hell..." she says. "I think I might have to call in sick to work today."

"I think that might be a good idea," I tell her, grinning.

Epilogue: Caroline, Two Months Later

I step outside, breathing in the fresh, morning mountain air. Samantha steps up behind me, wrapping her arms around my waist and bending down to rest her chin on my shoulder.

"You're sure you want to stay?" she asks.

"Yes, I'm sure," I tell her.

"Here?" she asks. "With me?"

We're standing in the backyard of her home, taking in the view of the surrounding trees. The summer camp has ended, the kids and staff are all headed home, and soon the heat will be retreating as autumn embraces the mountains.

I pivot inside her embrace, so we're face to face, and I tilt my head back to look up at her.

"Yes, here, with you," I tell her.

Everything has already been arranged. I got lucky and was able to get a job teaching at Blytheton High, the same high school we both attended. My parents are over the moon that I'm going to be back in Blytheton. Everything has seamlessly clicked into place. Sometimes I have to pinch myself, wondering how so much luck could be bestowed onto one person.

I rise up on my toes to kiss Samantha, but she bends down, meeting me halfway. It's a calm, patient kiss, both of us knowing we could take all the time in the world. I'm staying here with her. We've already moved my stuff from camp to her home. *Our* home. We're going to make a trip next week to Providence, so I can pack up the rest of my stuff. I'm excited to show Samantha around Providence, but I'm also excited to be leaving that life behind and starting a new one, with her. Samantha slowly pulls away from our kiss, and she brushes a few stray strands of hair from my face.

"Marry me?" she asks.

My heart skips a beat, but I smile up at her.

"Yes," I say, and pull her back down, demanding another kiss.

Thank you for reading! If you enjoyed this story, it would be greatly appreciated if you could leave a review on Amazon or Goodreads, even if it is just a star rating. Thank you!

ABOUT THE AUTHOR

Gemma (she/her) is a sapphic storyteller who enjoys writing steamy but sweet romance and spicy erotic romance.

If you liked this story, please consider following Gemma on Instagram & TikTok @gemma.addison.dove
For more information about Gemma and to sign-up for her newsletter, please visit: gemmaaddisondove.com
(or payhip.com/gemmaaddisondove)

BE SURE TO CHECK OUT WILD LOVE!

Available Now!

Cupcake baker Nelly needs to make it to her sister's cabin for her birthday, but grumpy mountain woman Lora is the only one available to drive her. When a storm causes a tree to fall and block their path, they're forced to take shelter in Lora's cozy cabin. And there's only one bed. *Wild Love* is a steamy sapphic instalove short romance featuring a thirty-two-year-old mountain woman falling for the sweetest girl in town.

This quick read includes:

- Sapphic romance/women loving women.

- Pansexual main character.

- Lesbian main character.

- Grumpy/Sunshine.

- Age gap romance (22/32).

- Best friend's little sister/Older sister's best friend.

- A cozy cabin with only one bed.

- V-card.

- Teach me vibes.

- Beater licking.

- Steamy scenes.

- Consent is sexy.

- Dual POV.

- Happily Ever After ending.

- And cupcakes.

Be Sure to Check Out: College Dorm Girls, Volume One

College Dorm Girls: Volume One is a collection of the first four short stories in the College Dorm Girls Collection.

First Time: Angel is a heavy sleeper - she even sleeps through her roommate's early morning lovemaking sessions. Little does she know, they wish she'd wake up and join them...But when she does, they realize this will be Angel's first time. Hailee and Olivia are more than happy to guide their friend.

Just Dinner, Part One: College student Jenny has been invited to dinner at Senator Gloria Graham's mansion. Jenny is on the autism spectrum and is nervous about the formal dinner, so her roommate Martina tags along. Jenny is unexpectedly outed as pansexual during the dinner, but Martina helps her cope; and tells Jenny that she's pan, too. The roommates had no idea they had both been pining for each other, but now they're ready to make up for lost time.

Just Dinner, Part Two: Jenny and Martina first met Vera, the senator's daughter, at an awkward dinner party. Vera goes to their college, and ever since the dinner, they keep bumping into her. The three girls decide it must be fate, especially since they're all interested in being more than friends.

Birthday Girl: It's Harper's birthday, and her girlfriends, Ava and Millie, have a special evening planned. There's going to be cake, strawberries, whipped cream, and...handcuffs. And it's going to be Harper's best birthday ever.

This is a collection of spicy sapphic short stories intended for mature audiences.

* 9 7 9 8 2 2 7 0 2 2 7 4 5 *